Mila and The Bear

Mila was a bright-eyed two-year old girl, with a huge imagination who loved riding her tricycle and was her happiest whenever she got to play with her friends from daycare.

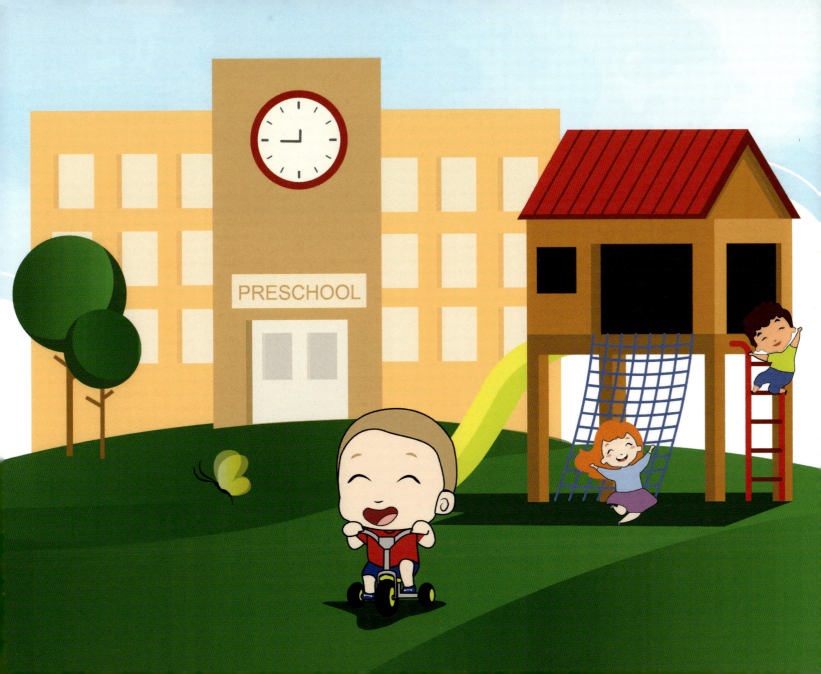

She was very sad when her parents told her they were moving because her dad got a new job. She really liked her friends and will miss them very much.

When Mila moved from the suburbs to the city, her parents gave her a bear so she would not feel alone because she had to say goodbye to her friends.

She was happy to have the bear and it soon became Mila's best friend, she took him everywhere. Soon summer came and went, which meant all the fun with her bear was coming to an end and school was soon to begin.

The first day of school had come and Mila was not thrilled. She cried and cried. When her parents asked why she was sad, Mila replied, "I'm going to be alone, I don't have any friends." Mila's mom told her the bear could go with her to school as long as it stayed in her book bag. And just like that Mila was happy again.

When Mila got to school, she went to put away her book bag and the bear tumbled out. When she picked up the bear, her two classmates, Camila in her red dress and Asha with her puff balls, quickly came over to check out the bear and introduced themselves.

The girls sat together during storytime. The teacher made an announcement that everyone can bring their favorite toy to storytime tomorrow. The girls' faces lit up with excitement and joy!

The next day, the girls formed an instant bond over their love for their furry friends.

Mila's first week of school was a success because even though her new friends looked different she realized they were just like her. She couldn't stop talking about her new friends at school and that night Mila told her bear "they'll be our friends forever."